SOFIA PROKOFIEVA

I Won't Apologize

Translated from the Russian by Raissa Bobrova
Drawings by G.A.W. Traugot

INSIGHT PUBLICA ®

Nadakkave, Kozhikode, Kerala
Tel:0495–4020666
www.insightpublica.com
e-mail: insightpublica@gmail.com
I Won't Apologize
Sofia Prokofieva
Translated by Raissa Bobrova
Drawings by G.A.W. Traugol
First Published by Raduga Publishers, Moscow USSR
Insight Publica Facsimile Edition : June 2020
Copyright©Reserved

ISBN 978-93-89804-71-3
Published by
Insightinpublica Publishers Pvt. Ltd.
Printed at Repro India Limited, India

Those fantastic
Soviet Books Again

All of us still have those fond memories of the books from the erst-while Soviet Union, which were once extensively circuated here, in Kerala - books of fabulous tales, riveting scientific facts and enchanting illustrations which stole the readers' hearts. They left in us an indelible impression and an unforgettable reading experience. An experience still ever-green in us, Malayali diaspora.

As the Union got dissolved, those charming books of tales too vanished, turning them into cherished memories of nostalgia. Yet, readers have relentlessly been looking for those inimitable books. That was why we, the INSIGHT PUBLICA, published a few of them in the same mode. We are grateful and glad to say that readers whole-heartedly backed us in realizing the project.

During the execution of our mission,we could fathom the depth and breadth of a great nation's remarkable literary project. Those sublime Soviet stories traversed in translation into many a nation and many a language. Those books were ubiquitous-not as merchandise, but as products of culture.

The fantastic bolstering that INSIGHT PUBLICA could get is the impetus that drove us daringly to undertake the mission of reprinting and republishing those Soviet works in Indian languages.

You readers need not anymore be discontented with the scanned copies of these books. INSIGHT PUBLICA will help reach into your hands those very books with the same freshness and warmth.

Let us present you again those fantastic Soviet Stories with humility and pride.

Sumesh Insight

CHAPTER ONE

There once lived a boy whose name was Vasya. He had a great many toys. They were everywhere in his room. Some were under the table, others under the wardrobe and still others under the bed.

But one morning Vasya woke up to find he wanted another toy, a rocking-horse.

"I want a rocking-horse," Vasya said.

"I want a rocking-horse!" Vasya shouted.

"I want a rocking-horse!!!" Vasya screamed and stamped his feet.

"Wait a bit, sonny," his Mummy said to him. "I have no money just now."

"No money?" Vasya yelled indignantly. "You have money for sugar. You have money for meat. You have money for potatoes and carrots... But you have no money for the most important thing. You are just mean, that's what you are!"

At that moment the wind threw open a window-pane, and a cold gust hit Vasya in the face. It carried prickly snow.

Mummy hastened to close the window, but it was already as cold in the room as it was outside in the street.

"You are a rude boy," Mummy said. "You ought to apologize for being so nasty to your mother."

"No, I won't apologize!" Vasya cried. He snatched his coat and hat and ran out of the house.

CHAPTER TWO

Vasya was sitting on a bench in the yard.

Thick snow was falling.

Vasya did not know that Freezing Cold had come to their city. It comes every time a boy or girl quarrels with his mother. The snow kept falling, and Vasya wondered how there could be so much of it up in the sky.

"Why should I apologize?" Vasya was thinking. "It's hateful. I'd rather never go home again..."

So Vasya went on sitting there, cold and miserable. Suddenly he saw a funny old man running in circles round the yard. The old man was wearing warm felt boots and a coat which looked unlike any boots and coat Vasya had ever seen. And an odd-looking fur cap.

"Why is he running like this?" Vasya wondered.

But he soon saw why. A black tom-cat was running about the yard like mad, while the old man was trying to catch it. The chase had obviously tired him, and Vasya felt sorry for the old man. On top of it, the black cat, as it galloped past Vasya, stopped for a second, gave him a look and put out a bright pink tongue.

"Teasing, are you?" Vasya gasped.

He jumped down from the bench and seized the cat by his hind legs in a fine dive. The cat was wet and slippery, but Vasya held him fast.

The old man ran over, snatched the cat out of Vasya's hands

and pushed it hurriedly into the bosom of his coat. After he regained his breath, he said very politely:

"Thank you for helping me catch this cat. I am not just any old man. I am Wizard, and this cat has magical power, too. It was extremely thoughtless of me to have taught him to cast spells. And now he no longer obeys me. He refuses to do anything useful and just keeps turning things into mice. He turned my writing desk into a mouse and ate it. He turned my bed into a mouse and gobbled it up as well. And this morning he turned the door of my flat into a mouse, caught it, swallowed it and ran out into the street. I've decided to go and ask the advice of Senior Wizard."

At this point the cat began to wriggle in the bosom of Wizard's coat and to mew:

"I'll turn everything into mice whatever you do!"

"Well, I must be off," Wizard said worriedly. He leaned down to Vasya and whispered into his ear:

"I must hurry up before it enters his head to turn *me* into a mouse. That would be extremely unpleasant, truth to say."

Wizard nodded to Vasya and walked off to the gate. Suddenly he stopped and came back.

"Vasya," he said, "I strongly advise you to go home and make up with your mother."

"What, apologize?" Vasya exploded. "Not for anything! It's hateful!"

"But a person cannot live without a mother," Wizard said.

"Why not?" Vasya muttered. "I might find myself a better one, too."

Wizard looked at Vasya thoughtfully.

"Very well," he said softly, "try it. And I shall do all I can to help you. Let's see what will come of it."

The snow started falling so thickly that Wizard disappeared from sight.

To be frank, Vasya did not want another mother at all. For his mother was not simply a mother, she was his very own special Mummy. In a word she was MUMMY.

But apologize? Not for anything.

Vasya sat on the bench a few minutes longer. His hands and feet were numb with cold, but the coldest of all, of course, was his nose. After all people have not invented anything like gloves or shoes to protect the nose from freezing.

And so his nose had become frozen hard like a cabbage stump. Vasya climbed down from the bench and went out of the yard. When he was already at the gate, the loudspeaker on the pole suddenly came to life:

"Attention! Attention! This is an alarm call!.."

But the wind howled and began to whirl madly, packing the black mouth of the loudspeaker with snow. The voice sounded weaker and weaker.

"Attention!.. An alarm call!.. A person has quarrelled with his mother! A person has quarrelled with his mother! This has happened in our home town. Now Freezing Cold has come to us! Citizens, protect your noses, ears and toes! Take care to shut the doors and windows. Attention! Attention! Freezing Cold has come to our town..."

But Vasya could no longer hear anything. Only the old sparrow who was sitting on the post made out a few words. He

became very upset, murmured something complainingly and flew off to tell the bad news to his wife. She must be warned never to leave the warm chimney side. Freezing Cold was not a thing to be trifled with.

CHAPTER THREE

Vasya walked along the street wondering why it had suddenly grown so cold. Only yesterday he had not even needed to wear his cap when he went outside.

At the street corner he saw a splendid dog. It was a Dachshund, so long it looked like a fat sausage on four legs.

Vasya even had a feeling that four legs were not enough for such a long dog. Another pair in the middle would be just right. The Dachshund was led on a leash by a woman in a gray fur-coat. As she passed Vasya, the woman suddenly whispered:

"Would you like me to be your Mummy?"

Vasya looked at the woman and thought that she seemed a good sort. And, most important, she had this wonderful long dog.

The woman and the dog stood waiting to hear what Vasya would say.

"Well, if I have to take a new Mummy, I might as well take one with a dog," he thought and said: "Okay."

Vasya said it in a low voice, so low that you could not be sure he said it at all. But Fierce Wind at once blew up with a roar and hard snow lashed Vasya's face.

The woman wrapped herself tighter in her gray fur-coat, seized Vasya's hand and ran like a hare down the street, saying:

"I have long wanted a little sonny like you. A curly-haired and snub-nosed sonny!"

The woman, the long dog and Vasya entered a house. But Fierce Wind forced its way in too. It became terribly cold on the staircase. The woman, the long dog and Vasya ran up the stairs to the first floor and entered one of the flats there.

"Oh, my!" The woman in the gray coat cried and waved her gray sleeves. "How stupid of me! I've forgotten to close the window! "What have I done!"

Indeed, the room they entered did not look like a room at all. There was a snowdrift on the sofa and another by the wardrobe. A pile of snow sat on the table. Snowflakes were darting about in the air. The long dog ran across the room, wading belly-deep in the snow.

"Never mind, sonny," said the woman in the gray coat. "We'll clean it all out in no time."

She brought in some pails and basins and they began carting the snow out of the room. But there was such a lot of it that however hard they worked there did not seem to become any less. The pails and basins grew ice-cold, and Vasya's hands became quite numb.

"We'll never clear the room of all this now, just the two of us," he thought miserably. "I'd need more mummies than one. Four or five at least."

Hardly had he thought this than four more women in gray fur-coats, exactly like the first one, entered the room. They were as like as peas in a pot. Vasya dropped the basin in astonishment.

"Why, are all these mummies for me alone?" he wondered. "But perhaps it's a good thing to have several mummies? Perhaps I'll get used to it?"

The women in gray coats started clearing the snow promptly. One swept it from under the sofa, another knocked down the icicles from the chandelier. The snowdrifts began to grow smaller very fast. The long dog could now run freely around the room.

"That's all, sonny," the women in gray coats said in a chorus and all smiled at Vasya.

"Come here, sonny, I'll give you a kiss," the woman nearest him said gently.

"Come here, sonny, I'll wipe your nose for you," said another.

"Have you forgotten your cod-liver oil, sonny?" said the third.

"Play with the dog while I get the supper ready," said the fourth.

"Take off your galoshes, sonny," said the fifth.

They all got hold of Vasya and started pulling him each to herself. Vasya's coat began to split at the seams. The long dog howled sadly.

Vasya broke free of them all and rushed out into the hall. The women in gray coats ran, bumping into one another, after him.

They caught up with him in the hall, surrounded him and spoke all at once. This is what he heard them say:

"Drink up the dog!"

"Play with the galoshes!"

"Take off your nose!"

"Kiss the cod-liver oil!"

Vasya covered his ears with his hands, ran out onto the landing and banged the door shut behind him.

"No, thank you," he muttered, horrified, "a person doesn't

need so many mothers. One has to love one's Mummy. But how can you love so many at once? You get all mixed up. No, I don't want..."

Suddenly all became quiet. There was only the sound of a woman's voice singing a merry song behind the door.

CHAPTER FOUR

Fierce Wind was sweeping the street. The street was a very long one, and the wind was long too.

Fierce Wind started playing tricks on Vasya, knocking off his hat, tugging at the ends of his scarf, raising the skirts of his coat. Vasya turned into a side street thinking it might not be so cold there.

But no! The moment Vasya turned round the corner, Fierce Wind began to howl there too and snow swirled in the air. The passers-by raised their collars and snuggled their noses in their scarfs. This made the noses break out in squares and stripes. And the children began to squeal and hop from the cold.

Vasya bent almost double and even covered his face with his coat sleeve. So he walked, seeing nothing, until he bumped into an ice-cream vendor, who was standing by a lovely blue box on little wheels.

"Ice-cream, ice-cream!" she shouted in a pleasant voice. "Chocolate, strawberry, vanilla!"

Vasya looked at the woman and saw at once that she was very nice, kind and cheerful.

MOPO HOT

"It must be fun to have your mother walk about the flat and say, 'Ice-cream! Ice-cream! Chocolate, strawberry, vanilla!'" he thought.

Vasya hung near the ice-cream vendor, but Fierce Wind seemed to be dogging Vasya's steps. It swirled round Vasya and the ice-cream woman, sprinkling them with prickly snow.

"Goodness!" the woman cried, trying to warm her hands by breathing on them. "Whoever will want my ice-creams in this nasty cold?"

"Would you like ... to be ... my..." Vasya whispered.

"Your mother?" the woman said joyfully as though she had been waiting for him to suggest it. She even stopped blowing on her fingers. "Yes, I'd like it very much. Right away!"

The ice-cream woman squatted and looked Vasya in the eye.

"But perhaps it's because of the ice-cream that you want me to be your mother?" she asked. "I wouldn't like that."

Vasya became hot with shame. He backed away from her, turned and fled along the street, past a snow-swept fence.

"Ice-cream! Chocolate! Strawberry! Vanilla!" he heard behind his back.

Vasya thought the woman's voice now sounded sad. She was a clever woman, and she had understood everything at once.

"No, one cannot choose a mummy like this," Vasya decided. "Not because of candy, nor because of cinema tickets... But I won't go home all the same. I'm not going to apologize."

The snow started falling so thickly that nothing could be seen around. Vasya's coat became white. And all of Vasya became white. Snow powdered his eyebrows and eyelashes.

For a long time he kept walking along endless streets and by-lanes, not knowing where.

"I must enter some house to get warm," he finally decided. "At least I can stand on a staircase."

But he could not see any houses, he could see nothing at all except big snowflakes dancing before his eyes and making him feel dizzy. And because of the frost he could not stand still ever for a minute. To get a little warmer, Vasya started to run.

He ran and ran until he crashed into a big tree. He looked round. All around him stood white trees.

CHAPTER FIVE

"I've got lost!" Vasya whispered. "What forest is this?"
It was even colder in the forest than it had been in the town.
Fierce Wind had swept together huge snowdrifts. Vasya was

extremely small, and the snowdrifts extremely big.

He wandered aimlessly among the drifts.

"Which way is the town?" thought Vasya. "What if I'm going deeper and deeper into the forest? There's nobody to ask. Just foxes and bears. I must turn back. Perhaps I can get out by following my own tracks?"

Vasya stopped and began to look round. But his tracks were no longer visible. Fierce Wind had covered them with snow.

It was cold standing, but if he walked on he might get lost altogether.

Vasya was frightened. And fear made him colder still.

Suddenly a big red Fox came out from behind a snowdrift.

Vasya could see that it was no ordinary fox, not the kind you see in a zoo.

Fox looked at Vasya and Vasya stared at Fox. Fox's eyes had a glint in them.

"I'd like a nice sonny," she suddenly said. "I am a very fine Fox, but I have no sonny."

"Gee, it talks!" Vasya thought with amazement.

He would probably be more amazed still had he not been so cold. He was frozen stiff, and his amazement was frozen stiff too.

Meanwhile the red Fox started walking around him, sweeping the snow with her handsome tail. Now and again she would curl it round a paw and it looked like a furry cuff. Then she would lay it on her neck and it would be like a fluffy collar.

"If I had a sonny, I'd make him some nice porridge," Fox said, looking to the side.

"Shall I go with her perhaps," Vasya wondered, shiver-

ing with cold. "I'll get warm and have some porridge besides."

Fox seemed to guess his thoughts.

"That's right, my little one, come along. We'll gather some firewood in a moment and go home. Stretch out your arms and I'll load the sticks on them. Here, logs, sticks, chips and twigs..." Fox sang out, as she loaded firewood on Vasya's outstretched arms. She put more and more until he all but swayed under its weight and had to hold the last chip in place with his chin.

"Come on, sonny," said Fox. "You'll carry the firewood half the way, and I'll carry it the other half. See that birch-tree over there? That'll be exactly half the way."

Finally they reached the birch-tree.

"Oh, sonny, I'm sorry," Fox said with a sigh. "This isn't half the way yet, I was mistaken. We'll have gone half the way when we get to that old oak-tree over there. Carry the load some more."

Vasya carried the firewood as far as the oak-tree, and Fox said.

"No, sonny, not yet, half the way will be by that pine. Carry it a bit more."

By the time they reached the pine Vasya could barely hold the heavy load. He was dead tired and felt as though his arms might be pulled out of their sockets.

"Here, this is my house," Fox laughed craftily.

Indeed, a fox house, all painted red, stood under the pine. It had a red door, a red roof and red windows and chimney.

"Why did you have to fool me?" Vasya asked tearfully. "I'd have carried the firewood all the way to your house if you asked me."

Fox was put out and rubbed her nose with a paw.

"Forgive me, sonny, I'll never deceive you again. Come on in, let's cook that porridge."

Vasya took the firewood into the house and dropped the load by the stove.

Fox's house was an old one, and Fierce Wind made its way in through the chinks, sweeping snow inside.

Fox began to make the porridge in a red pot. Soon the milk came to a boil, the porridge began to bubble, spreading a delicious smell. It became warmer in the house. Fox took a big spoonful of porridge, blew on it and pushed into her mouth.

"No, it's not ready yet," she said, licking the spoon clean. She stirred the porridge and tasted it again. She kept tasting it, eating one spoonful after another and saying each time it was not properly cooked yet.

Vasya looked into the pot and saw there was hardly any porridge left. Fox had eaten it all. Once again Fox was ashamed and covered her face with her tail.

"Oh, sonny, I've deceived you again! I simply can't help it. Deceit is my second nature. It's the way I've been born."

Tears welled up in Vasya's eyes.

"And you want to be somebody's mummy? You think it is easy to be a mummy? Mummy never cheats or deceives! No, you won't make a mummy, never!"

"No," Fox said sadly, "it doesn't look as though I shall."

Vasya ran out of the house, down the steps and away across untrodden snow.

"What a fool I am," he was thinking. "I knew right away that I'll never find myself another mummy. I'll never get used to any other. But I won't apologize all the same. I'll live alone."

Fierce Wind began to howl and whine and screech trying to frighten Vasya. And it was really frightening, even though Vasya could not make out any words.

"Ooooo," said Fierce Wind. "Pssszt!"

Vasya nearly doubled up against the wind, raised his collar, pushed his hands into his sleeves. Suddenly there was a crackling of branches, and a furry mountain on four big paws walked out of some bushes. Vasya recognized it at once—it was She-Bear.

"Are you looking for a mummy?" She-Bear asked in a deep voice.

"No, no," Vasya said, his teeth chattering. "I have a mummy, I have..."

"Why don't you live with me and be my sonny? My flat is so too big for me alone."

"Can I come and visit you, without becoming your sonny?" Vasya whispered.

"Very well then," She-Bear agreed. "I'll give you supper and put you to bed."

So Vasya trudged after She-Bear.

"Step in my tracks, that'll make it easier going," she advised.

But her tracks were as deep as pits. When Vasya tried stepping into one, his leg went down up to the thigh.

"Here's home," She-Bear said at last.

Vasya looked and could not see any house. Before him was a huge snowdrift with a black hole leading underground. Well, there was nothing for it, and Vasya crawled through the hole following She-Bear.

"Here is the corridor," she said, "and here is my room. Come on in, don't be shy."

Vasya buttoned up his coat and crouched in the corner. She-Bear cut off a big chunk of bread and poured some golden honey over it.

The honey flowed off the bread. When Vasya bit on one side, the honey dripped from the other, so Vasya had to hurry and lick it off.

She-Bear sat leaning her furry back against the wall and yawning.

"Ooogh!" she yawned. "Winter came early this year."

She opened her mouth wide, and Vasya was scared at the sight of the huge maw and the many big teeth.

She-Bear noticed Vasya's frightened look and began to cover up her mouth with her paw when she yawned. She was a good sort, that She-Bear, tactful and kind.

Vasya ate up the bread and honey. His hands were sticky and he could hardly keep his eyes open, either because of the sticky honey or because he felt sleepy.

He kept looking at She-Bear and finally started yawning too.

"Hrrr," suddenly She-Bear fell on her side and began to snore. She was fast asleep. Again she looked like a furry mountain. One could not tell where was the front and where the back.

"Wake up, She-Bear," Vasya cried in fear. "What shall I do here, all alone?"

"What is it?" asked She-Bear drowsily. "Why, go to sleep, too. We shall sleep a long time now. Till spring." And she began to snore again.

"What do you mean till spring?" Vasya cried in alarm. "I don't want to sleep so long!"

He poked She-Bear's furry side, but she did not even stir.

"See!" Vasya whispered reproachfully. "Mummy always puts me to bed first, and only then goes to sleep herself. And she never sleeps all the winter through."

Vasya felt lost sitting by the sleeping She-Bear.

"I can't sit like this till spring," he said to himself. And he crawled out of the bear den.

CHAPTER SIX

It was already night in the forest.

The snowdrifts were so big they looked black.

Vasya sunk up to his waist in the deep snow, and barely managed to get out. But when he did, he noticed his galoshes were gone. The snowdrift had pulled them off and hid them. Vasya began rummaging in the snow, trying to find the galoshes, and the snowdrift pulled his mittens off and hid them as well.

Vasya was now really in trouble. He crawled through the snow to a tall fir-tree.

"Fir-tree," he whispered, "see I am all alone in the forest, without my Mummy. Cover me with your branches, please."

Old Fir-Tree lifted its branches creakingly and Vasya crawled underneath them and pressed his back to the trunk. And there he sat, rolled into a ball. Fir-Tree lowered its thick branches and covered Vasya with them.

"How prickly you are," Vasya whispered. "Mummy has not one prickle."

But Freezing Cold was not going to leave Vasya in peace. It made its way under Fir-Tree, creeping through between the needles.

Fir-Tree started to hum as though it was full of pipes.

"Is it calling someone?" Vasya wondered.

Fir-Tree trumpeted again.

Suddenly the branches were parted, and somebody breathed warmly right into Vasya's face. Vasya looked and saw a horse's big head and a sad eye fixed on him.

"I'm so cold," Vasya whispered. "Breathe on me again, please."

"You're in a bad way, boy," Horse said worriedly. "Better crawl out of there and get on my back. You'll freeze to death here."

It took Vasya a long time to climb on Horse's back, so stiff he was from cold. Horse trotted among the trees, while Vasya wrapped his hands in her mane, buried his face into it and closed his eyes. Horse came to her horsy home, went up the stairs to the porch and into the room.

Her house was big and solid, but quite empty. There was no furniture, just a big heap of hay in the corner. Vasya looked at Horse and saw she was very old and sad. Her eyes were sad, and she had a sad white spot on the forehead.

"Are you hungry?" Horse asked sadly.

"I'm cold," Vasya answered.

Horse made him a bed on the heap of hay and covered him with an old horse-cloth. She tucked him in carefully, but Vasya did not feel any warmer.

"I didn't know horses lived in the forest," he said.

Horse shook her head sadly.

"I used to live on a collective farm," she said. "But then the farm bought a tractor, and I saw I was no longer needed. I went off to town and found a job at the bakery. I carted loaves and tasty rolls to bakery shops. But the manager of the bakery bought a lorry, and I saw he did not need me either. Then I

went off into the forest, built this house and began living here. But I shall probably die soon. What's the point of living when nobody needs you."

"And who needs me?" Vasya wondered. "Mummy does!"

Horse looked away. She probably did not want Vasya to see her sad eyes.

"Nobody is waiting for me... Nobody is thinking about me... Nobody is worried..." Horse muttered mournfully under her breath.

"Mummy is worried about me," Vasya thought. "Of course she is worried. She does not know where I am. She must be out of her mind with worry. My Mummy."

"Horse, my dear Horse," Vasya said tearfully. "Please, take me home! As fast as you can. To Mummy. Because Mummy is worried!"

Horse looked out the window and shook her head.

"Look at this snowstorm. Listen to the wind howling. I don't remember such a terrible night in our forest. You will freeze to death. I'll never get you home alive. Let's wait till morning, shall we?"

"No, I must go today! Now, right now!" Vasya cried. "Mummy is worried!"

"All right, don't cry," Horse said. "If it's so important, I'll take you to your mother."

Vasya climbed on Horse's back, and she walked down the steps carefully.

The blizzard rushed at them eagerly. It howled, and it circled around them. It swirled the snow and dashed it into

their eyes and faces, now from the right, now from the left. It would not let them out of the forest. Horse walked very slowly, swaying and stumbling at every step.

"What's the matter with you, Horse?" Vasya asked in alarm. "Are you ill? You aren't going to die, are you?"

"No, I am just sad, very, very sad," Horse said. "I keep thinking that nobody needs me."

"But it's not true, Horse!" Vasya cried. "You *are* needed, very much so! *I* need you! Without you I'd have frozen to death in this forest. I cannot make you my mummy, because I already have Mummy, who I love very much. But you will always be my very best friend."

Horse lifted her head and began to trot. Obviously Vasya's words had cheered her up.

Soon she reached the town.

All the windows in the town were dark, because all the children, and their mothers too, were asleep.

In one street Vasya saw Wizard, who was walking with a weary step, carrying the black cat.

Wizard was overjoyed to see them.

"Stop! Stop!" he cried. "All the trams are asleep in their parks, and so are all the trolleybuses. Please, give us a lift, we're going the same way."

"You're welcome," said Horse.

Wizard climbed on Horse's back and sat behind Vasya, holding on to him with one hand.

"Are you going home to your mother?" Wizard asked.

"Yes," said Vasya.

At that point he noticed that it had become much warmer, and that Fierce Wind was no longer blowing. Snow was melting and hundreds of tiny brooks were murmuring all around them.

"Did Senior Wizard help you?" Vasya asked.

"Yes," said Wizard. "It all proved to be very simple. I should have thought of it myself, as a matter of fact. Senior Wizard and I turned all the things in his flat into mice. And these mice attacked my cat. The tea-kettle-mouse began to pour boiling water over him. The vacuum-cleaner-mouse began to pull at his fur. The flat-iron-mouse sat down on his tail. The salt-cellar-mouse sprinkled him with salt. And baby tooth-brush-mouse began to clean his teeth. They drove him mad, and he gave a word of cat's honour never to turn things into mice again. Unless somebody asks him very hard."

"Perhaps you can turn me into something useful?" Horse asked sadly.

"Into a mouse?" the cat asked eagerly. "Some horses have the same colour as mice."

"No, I don't want to be a mouse," Horse said miserably.

After that they drove in silence for a long time. Vasya was tired and leaned against Wizard's chest.

Suddenly Vasya saw light in one window. It was, of course, Vasya's house. And the lighted window was, of course, in Vasya's room. Vasya jumped down from Horse, hugged her neck and whispered into her ear:

"Don't go away, please. I'll be back in a moment."

And he rushed home.

Mummy opened the door. She was very pale and her eyes were red.

"Where have you been all this time?" she asked. "I was so worried. Really, Vasya..."

Vasya threw himself into her arms, crying:

"Mummy, please forgive me!"

And he saw that it was quite easy — to apologize and ask to be forgiven. It was easy, and nice and even comforting.

Mummy kissed Vasya, and he at once felt as warm as warm can be, because at that moment Freezing Cold left the town.

"Mummy," Vasya said, "I left a very nice Horse outside in the yard. She is my friend. Can I take her in?"

"Of course," Mummy said.

"And she will live with us, may she?"

"Very well," said Mummy. "But I don't know whether she will like it here. Of course I can get hay and oats for her. But will she like riding in the lift? And walking five flights of stairs will be hard on her."

Vasya ran out into the yard, and saw a wooden rocking-horse with a white spot on her forehead standing by the door.

The wooden horse was rocking and smiling.

"Has Wizard done that?" Vasya asked.

The rocking-horse nodded.

Vasya clutched the horse to his chest and ran home. At home he hugged his mummy, kissed her and rubbed his nose against her cheek.

And then Vasya went to bed.

Mummy put out the light.

Beside his bed a wooden rocking-horse kept rocking and smiling.